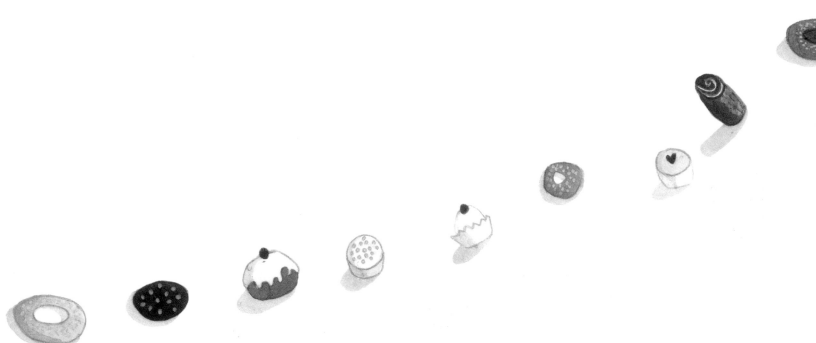

For Rosemary Canter, with love – S.P.
For Rose, with love – H.S.

First published in Great Britain and in the USA in 2006 by
Frances Lincoln Children's Books, 4 Torriano Mews,
Torriano Avenue, London NW5 2RZ

Distributed in the USA by Publishers Group West

www.franceslincoln.com

British Library Cataloguing in Publication Data available on request

Set in Blockhead
Illustrated with concentrated watercolour
and coloured pencil

ISBN 10: 1-84507-475-0
ISBN 13: 978-1-84507-475-3

Printed in Singapore
1 3 5 7 9 8 6 4 2

MISS FOX

Simon Puttock

Illustrated by Holly Swain

F

FRANCES LINCOLN
CHILDREN'S BOOKS

Welcome to Niceville

It was the first day of school
when Miss Fox, substitute teacher, strolled into Niceville.
It looked like a comfy sort of, cosy sort of place,
so she stopped and asked a kindly storekeeper
the way to Niceville School.

Miss Fox smiled her sweetest smile at Mr Billy, the head teacher.

"I am the most wonderful teacher in the world," she told him. "You NEED me to teach your dear little children."

Of course, Mr Billy hired Miss Fox on the spot.

"Pay attention, Class Two. I am Miss Felicity Fox, and I am a WONDERFUL teacher."

"Ooh!" gasped everyone in Class Two. Everyone, that is, except Lily Lamb.

Lily Lamb was a headstrong girl who always asked annoying questions and never EVER would be told what to do.

"Bah!" said Lily. "Silly old Foxy! Who does she think she is?" And she went on making paper aeroplanes.

But Miss Fox WAS a wonderful teacher. Every day she brought the children treats: doughnuts, cream buns and, of course, little cakes with pink icing.

"Miss Fox is the BEST," Class Two agreed, "and truly supreme!"

"Bah!" said Lily Lamb. "You're all just greedy-weedies. Miss Fox never eats treats herself. I wonder what she does like to eat...?"

At playtimes, Miss Fox kept the children indoors
and told them tales of kind, beautiful, noble foxes
doing wonderful things.

"Ooh!" said Class Two. "TERRIFIC STORY!"

"Bah! Bah — soppy!" said Lily Lamb.

FOXES THROUGH HISTORY

1 2

And she   sneaked out   to play   hopscotch   all by

herself.

Everyone in Class Two was happy
and well fed – and lazy. Everyone, that is,
except Lily Lamb. She stayed just as cross
and annoying and nimble as ever.

On the last morning of term, Miss Fox clapped her hands. "Children," she said, "you have all been SO good that today we are going for a nice, long nature walk. Now, I am the leader, so form a line and follow me!"

"we'd follow you ANY

"Bah!" said Lily Lamb. "Bah, silly old Foxy! I am a free spirit and I WILL NOT BE LED!"

SCHOOL

iceville

Class Two followed Miss Fox out of the playground and across the road and over the fields and into the woods

and through the trees, all the way to the top of a great tall cliff.

And Lily Lamb skipped from side to side, being a muddle and a mess at the end of the line.

"Now, gather round," said Miss Fox,
smiling her most dazzling smile.
"You are such SWEET children..."
    (She took a napkin from her handbag.)
    "...and I'm sure you're all delicious.
So who wants to be first to be eaten?"
    "Hee, hee!" everyone giggled.
Isn't Miss Fox funny?"
    Everyone, that is, except Lily Lamb.
She KNEW Miss Fox meant business.

                            So...

"I will be first," said Lily Lamb.

"Why, Lily!" said Miss Fox. "You've decided to be good at last. You couldn't possibly taste as sweet as some, but do come quickly, for I am VERY hungry."

"But please tell me," said Lily Lamb, "will you eat me up snip-snap, just so?"

"I will gobble you up in a bite!" said Miss Fox.

"And are you sure," asked Lily, "you can manage us ALL?"

"Every single one of you," said Miss Fox. "Wonderful teachers do NOT have favourites. Now, Lily Lamb,

COME

HERE

AND

BE

EATEN!"

"Eek!" gasped Class Two. "We do believe that Miss Fox really means it!" And everyone began to tremble. Everyone, that is, except Lily Lamb.
"All right, Miss Fox," said Lily. "I'm ready, but you'd better open wide."

"Just you jump
to it, Lily Lamb,
for I am

STARVING!"

Miss Fox closed her eyes
and opened her mouth as wide
as it would go.
'Now's my chance,'
thought Lily,
and with a rush
and a push
and a shove
and a heave
and a puff
and a pant.

...she sent Miss Fox

tumbling over the cliff.

"Goodbye, Foxy!"
she shouted.
"Being good is SO boring,
don't you agree?"

"Ooh! How true," said Class Two.
"You ARE brave, Lily Lamb."
"Aren't I just!" said Lily, smiling
her best and most mischievous smile.

It was the first day of school
when Miss Fox strolled into Pleasant Town.
It looked like a comfy sort of, cosy sort of place.

YOU ARE NOW LEAVING PLEASANT TOWN

Miss Fox licked her lips
and smiled her prettiest smile.